Chloe's Secret Fairy Godmother Club

Scholastic Children's Books
An imprint of Scholastic Ltd
Euston House, 24 Eversholt Street, London, NW1 1DB, UK
Registered office: Westfield Road, Southam, Warwickshire, CV47 0RA
SCHOLASTIC and associated logos are trademarks and/or
registered trademarks of Scholastic Inc.

First published in the UK by Scholastic Ltd, 2017

Text copyright © Emma Barnes, 2017
Cover illustration copyright © Monique Dong, 2017
Inside illustrations by Mike Love

The right of Emma Barnes, Mike Love and Monique Dong
to be identified as the author and illustrators of this work has
been asserted by them.

ISBN 978 1407 16449 6

A CIP catalogue record for this book
is available from the British Library.

Printed by CPI Group (UK) Ltd, Croydon, CR0 4YY
Papers used by Scholastic Children's Books are made
from wood grown in sustainable forests.

1 3 5 7 9 10 8 6 4 2

This is a work of fiction. Names, characters, places, incidents
and dialogues are products of the author's imagination or are used
fictitiously. Any resemblance to actual people, living or
dead, events or locales is entirely coincidental.

www.scholastic.co.uk

Chloe's Secret Fairy Godmother Club

Emma Barnes

Illustrated by Mike Love

SCHOLASTIC

♥ Chapter One ♥

It all started with Eliza's big secret. Not that we knew at first she *had* a secret. For a long time all that Aisha (my other best friend) and me knew was that Eliza was acting really strangely.

Eliza, Aisha and I usually spend *all* our time together. We play together and line up together and walk around the playground arm in arm together and we are always going round to each other's houses. At school, if

1

our teacher tells us to do something in pairs, then we always stick up our hands and say, "Please, Mr Carter, can't we work as a three? We'll be good, we promise."

Mr Carter usually rolls his eyes, and says, "You three! Anyone would think you were glued together!" But if he's in a good mood, he says, "Go on, then! You can be the ACE Team." He calls us that because of the first letters of our names: Aisha, Chloe, Eliza. He thinks it is a good joke.

Sometimes he adds, "At least Aisha and Eliza can keep an eye on Chloe. Chloe needs two people to keep her feet on the ground."

What he means by this is that I am a bit of a dreamer. My dad calls me Chloe-in-the-clouds because I am always drifting off. The trouble is, I get carried away and stop listening in class and instead imagine that

there's an alien on the roof or an assassin has poisoned school dinners or the caretaker's cat has evil powers and used to belong to a witch. And I tell everyone else to hide or not to eat their school dinner or to watch out for that cat … then the next thing is I'm being sent to Mrs Khan, the head teacher, and she's shaking her head and saying, "It's time you learned to keep

3

your feet on the ground, Chloe."

The best thing Aisha, Eliza and me ever did was invent our Secret Club. We turned ourselves into the three princesses, Clarinda, Araminta and Elizabetta, and had lots of adventures. We are always looking for exciting things to do.

But lately things had changed. Eliza hadn't been her usual self. She was really quiet at school. Whenever Aisha and I suggested something new for our club to do, she just shrugged. And sometimes she would go off and just sit by herself in the playground and gaze moodily out through the railings.

She didn't want to play Tag. Or go on the climbing structure. Or even play her trumpet in the school band. It wasn't like Eliza at all.

One day at break time, Mr Carter told Aisha and me to take the register to the office. Afterwards, we looked for Eliza. We searched and searched, but we couldn't find her anywhere.

She wasn't in our favourite spot under the big chestnut tree.

She wasn't in the girls' toilets.

She wasn't on the climbing structure.

She had vanished.

"Where can she be?" asked Aisha. "Do you think she's gone home?"

"Why would she do that?"

"Maybe she's sick. She looks so sad, like she's got a bad tummy."

"But she's looked like that for days," I pointed out. "Or not sad exactly, but quiet and—"

"Gloomy chops," Aisha said.

I nodded. "It's not like Eliza."

We looked at each other anxiously.

"She still can't have vanished," said Aisha.

And then my imagination began to whirr. What if Eliza was really unhappy? What if she didn't like being at school with us any more? What if she'd seen a bus stopping outside our playground? And she'd decided to leap on board...

"Maybe she's run away!" I jumped to my feet. "Come on, Aisha! We have to go after her!"

I was all ready to rush to the school gates. Aisha grabbed my arm.

"Chloe, don't be silly. Of course she hasn't run away!"

"How do you know?"

"Because somebody would have seen her."

"Then where is she?"

"I don't know, but we'll find her if we look hard enough."

So we started searching all over again.

6

We looked everywhere. We even crawled underneath the benches in the cloakroom. We found three toffees and my lost gym shoe. But Eliza was nowhere to be seen.

"This is awful," I said to Aisha. "We'd better tell Mr Carter. And he can call the police and look at the bus timetables just in case she has run away and—"

I stopped. I'd just noticed something out of the corner of my eye. A flash of red. Somebody was in the school greenhouse!

"Look!" I hissed to Aisha.

Aisha said, "But we're not allowed in there. You know we're not."

You're only allowed in the school greenhouse if you're doing Garden Club. Mrs Khan made that rule after some boys were messing about and broke a flowerpot.

"I'm sure it's her," I said, bending over sideways, trying to see in. "That's her cardigan. Come on! After all, it's an emergency!"

Aisha looked a bit unsure, but she followed me into the greenhouse. There, half-hidden among the marigolds and baby lettuces, was … Eliza.

"Oh, hello," she said gloomily. "It's you."

Her shoulders were hunched and her mouth drooped. She looked as mopey as a mopey thing.

"What's wrong?" I asked.

"*Nothing.*"

"You don't look very cheerful."

Eliza sniffed. It was rather a sad sniff. Like the kind of sniff that meant she was about to cry.

"You can tell us," Aisha said gently. "We're here to help."

"Of course we are," I agreed. "After all, that is what our Secret Club is all about.

8

We have to stick up for each other."

A tear trickled down Eliza's cheek. She got out a tissue and wiped it away quickly, but we'd both seen. And it wasn't like Eliza to start crying.

We sat down on either side of her and each put an arm round her.

"It's OK, Eliza."

"Don't worry!"

"We'll sort it out!"

Already my imagination was working overtime. What if Eliza was going away? A few weeks ago her dad had gone on a business trip to Australia. He'd really liked it there, Eliza had said. What if her parents had decided

to move there? Poor Eliza would get on a plane and Aisha and I would be left behind. Maybe we'd never see her again. She would be having barbecues on the beach or making friends with wallabies, and Aisha and me would be stuck here.

"We'll still be best friends!" I burst out. "And we'll save all our pocket money and come and visit you in Australia!"

Aisha and Eliza stared at me. Eliza said, "Why are you talking about Australia?"

"Oh – because, I thought – well, what *is* the matter then?"

Eliza gave a big sniff. "Mum's having a baby. I'm going to have a new brother or sister – and I don't want one!"

Chapter Two

We stared at her in amazement.

"Why do they want to have a baby?" I asked.

"Exactly," said Eliza. "I mean, there's always just been me. Me and Hercules." (Hercules is Eliza's dog.) "When I was little sometimes I thought I'd like to have a sister or brother. But now I'm used to it being me, and I like it!"

Aisha and I looked at each other. We've

11

both got brothers, so we know how awful they can be. I've got Arthur, my twin, and Aisha is even worse off – she's got three! So it was hard to know what to say.

"Maybe it will be fun," I suggested. "Maybe you'll like the baby when it arrives."

"Babies just cry a lot," Eliza said. "And their nappies smell."

Aisha nodded sadly. "It's true. That's *exactly* what they do." (Aisha's three brothers are all younger than her.) "Also," Aisha went on, "they make a mess and they crawl about, and once they're big enough they get hold of your stuff and break it, and—"

I gave her a little poke in the shoulder with one finger, and when she looked at me I made a face. It was a face that was meant to say, *you're not helping*.

"I bet this baby will be sweet," I said

firmly. I was determined to cheer Eliza up. "And it might be a girl. I bet a little sister's better than a brother."

"After all," said Aisha, "it couldn't be *worse*."

I poked her again.

Eliza said, "But I won't even know until it's born, because Mum and Dad don't want to find out. They want it to be a surprise."

"Well, that's another thing," I said, looking on the bright side. "You've got plenty of time to get used to the idea, before the baby arrives."

"Nine months," Aisha put in helpfully. "That's how long it takes."

"Not this time," Eliza wailed. "Because this baby was a surprise to Mum and Dad too! They didn't tell me straight off – and now, well, I expect it won't be that long before the baby's here!"

Eliza was so worked up that she waved her arms and a marigold pot fell over, *clump*, and she didn't even notice.

"Mum and Dad keep going on and on about this baby. Dad's been singing yucky songs to Mum's bump! He calls the baby his little dumpling – *I* used to be his dumpling. All they can talk about is which name and which pram. We can't even go on holiday any more, because of the baby. We were meant to go to Disney!"

Aisha and I looked solemn. Losing out on a trip to Disney World was pretty serious.

Eliza said, "And when I grumbled, they said it was a shame but 'a little brother or sister is better than Disney, isn't it?'" Eliza scowled. "*I* don't think it is."

"That's grown-ups for you," Aisha said. "They have the strangest ideas. My parents are always saying how lucky I am to have three brothers!"

"And mine think Arthur and I are so lucky to be twins," I put in. "It's *rubbish* being twins. We even have to be in the same class at school." (Actually, I don't hate being a twin. Well, not *all* the time. But I thought it would make Eliza feel better.)

"They used to say it was perfect, just me and Hercules," said Eliza. "And now they've forgotten us." She scrubbed her eyes. "I think Hercules is quite hurt. I have to spend a lot of time telling him he's a good dog."

We fell silent. At least Eliza looked happier now she had shared her secret. She'd stopped crying.

"I wish *you* were getting new babies too," she said suddenly. "We'd all be in it together. And we could help each other."

15

"We'll still help you," I told her. "We'll pretend we're big sisters too."

"We'll be a bit like aunties," said Aisha.

"You're too young," said Eliza.

"No, we're not," Aisha said. "One of my aunties is thirteen. That's not much older than us."

It was then I had the most wonderful idea. "No, better than that! We'll be its fairy godmothers!"

Aisha and Eliza just gazed at me with their mouths open in astonishment. They looked like a pair of goldfishes.

"FAIRY GODMOTHERS?"

"Yes!" I jumped up. I was so excited I couldn't sit still. "Like in *Sleeping Beauty*. Don't you remember? All the good fairies came to visit Sleeping Beauty when she was born, and they used their magic to give her special gifts, like wisdom and kindness and ... and ... well, you know the kind of thing!"

I had a picture in my head. The new baby was lying in a fancy crib, with long lacy curtains hanging down, and a sweet little smile on its face. Aisha and Eliza and I were leaning over it with our wands. We wore fairy crowns and long dresses and butterfly wings. "I give you the gift of happiness!" I cried, as I tapped the crib with my wand...

I came back to earth to find Aisha and Eliza still gawping at me. "What gift of happiness?" asked Eliza.

"Yes, you're not making much sense, Chloe," said Aisha.

I could feel my cheeks getting hot. "What I mean is ... why can't we be fairy godmothers?"

"Wouldn't we need to know magic?" asked Aisha doubtfully.

17

"We can make it up as we go along!"

Aisha loves fairy tales. I could see my idea was growing on her. She nodded.

Eliza looked interested too. Eliza loves pretty clothes and sparkly things and dressing up. She said, "Perhaps I'd feel better about the baby if I could be a fairy godmother. I can be one as well as a big sister, can't I?"

"Definitely."

Hmm," she said. "Of course, in *Sleeping Beauty* there's also a *bad* fairy..."

"Well, we're going to be the *good* kind," I said quickly. I didn't want Eliza trying to turn the baby into a pig or making it fall asleep for a hundred years.

"I love it!" said Aisha. "Maybe I can put a spell on my brothers. One that makes them stay out of my room!"

We all laughed.

"*That* will take some powerful magic!" I said.

19

"But what I want to know," said Eliza, "is what we are going to do *now*? I mean do we have to wait until the baby's born?"

"Of course we don't!" I was getting more and more excited. "Don't you see? We need something new for our club to do. And this is it! We can be the Secret Fairy Godmother Club!"

Chapter Three

Of course, after that we couldn't think of *anything* but fairy godmothers. That afternoon, we were supposed to be doing maths, and Mr Carter told me off for drawing stars when I was supposed to be drawing isosceles triangles. I wasn't the only one either. Aisha's triangles ended up looking like fairy wings, and when Mr Carter asked Eliza how you know something is a triangle, she said dreamily, "Because it has three wishes."

21

Every time I caught Aisha or Eliza's eyes across the classroom we would give each other a secret smile or wink. Eliza was looking happier – almost her old self. At one point she did a little flutter with her hand, as if she was pretending to scatter fairy dust.

"You know, Chloe," Rachel said, "You'd do a lot better if you just kept your mind on your work." Rachel sits at my table, which is my bad luck, because she is the sort of person who behaves perfectly and always gets things right. Also, she thinks it's her job to tell everyone what they should be doing, as if she's the teacher.

Of course, I didn't tell her about being fairy godmothers. I just shrugged.

"And another thing," Rachel went on, "I couldn't help noticing you were in the greenhouse today. I'm sure you know that's out of bounds. I hope it's not going to happen again."

Luckily, at that moment, Barney, who is one of Arthur's friends and a right pain, fell backwards off his chair. This meant that Rachel could enjoy herself telling *him* off instead.

When I got home, I didn't even go and get a snack with Arthur the way I normally do. Instead I rushed upstairs and started searching through my dressing-up box. I was sure I had a pair of fairy wings – and a wand too – but I couldn't find them anywhere. I even looked in Arthur's room (which made him mad) and then I tipped my whole dressing-up box upside down on my carpet to check.

I had all kinds of useless things – like the ladybird costume I'd worn to my fifth birthday party, and a pair of Rudolph the Red-Nosed Reindeer antlers that flash when you press a button. But no wand and no fairy wings.

"Do you know where they've gone?" I asked Hammy, my hamster, who was peering curiously at me from his cage.

Hammy scrunched up his nose at me.

"No, I suppose not."

I sat back on my heels and thought. Then I yelled at the top of my voice, "MUM!" and went shooting on to the landing.

"Chloe?" Her voice came from her bedroom so I zoomed in there.

"MUM! I've just *got* to have a wand and wings! It's urgent! You must take me to buy them! Like, now, this minute, straight away!"

"Chloe!" Mum was lying on her bed.

"Do you have to make such a racket?"

"What's the matter?"

"I have a headache so I'm having a rest before tea." Mum paused. "Well, I *was* having a rest, until—"

"Sorry. I didn't mean to wake you up. I just wondered if we could go somewhere that sells wands and fairy wings? Because I absolutely need them."

Mum groaned. I guess her headache was really bad.

"You see, it's essential!" I added, just in case she hadn't got the message.

Mum shut her eyes tight. Then she opened them again. "Wands and wings are *not* essentials, Chloe. You can put them on your birthday list."

"But it's ages until my birthday!"

"Then how about making some? And now," Mum added firmly, "I'm going to

25

try and get a bit of a sleep."

She turned over. I went back to my room and put Hammy in his special exercise ball. It's made of clear plastic, so Hammy can see out. It rolls along the floor as Hammy runs about.

"Maybe it's not a headache," I said to Hammy. "Maybe it's something else. Like … maybe Mum's going to have a baby too?" Hammy looked at me and wrinkled his nose. I could tell he didn't agree. It was as if he was saying, "Don't be silly. Your mum always says you and Arthur are quite enough, thank you very much!"

"I suppose you're right," I admitted. "And I'm not sure I want a baby brother or sister really." I thought some more. "Do you know what would be really cute, Hammy? A hamster baby! It wouldn't take up much room either. And then you'd have company when I was at school."

I could see it now – a darling little baby hamster, with golden fur and a ribbon round its neck. Hammy would look after it. He would lick its fur and, when it got bigger, he would teach it to play on his wheel or run around in his exercise ball.

I thought about going to tell Mum my good idea. Then I decided not to. You never know with mums. They might not see things the same way. Something told me I should wait for a better moment before saying anything about hamster babies.

I looked at my heap of dressing-up clothes. "I still want fairy wings, though," I told Hammy. "Mum said I should try making some. What do you reckon, Hammy? Shall I have a go?"

I thought Hammy nodded. Or it might have been his whiskers bobbing, but it was good enough for me.

I put Hammy back in his cage so he could watch.

"I need cardboard," I told Hammy. "This box I was using for my dressing-up stuff will do. And I need scissors. And elastic to tie them on. Only I don't have any elastic ... I know! I'll use my tights. And felt tips pens to make them pretty. And lots of twinkly stuff and glitter ... I'll need glue too. Hmm – what have I done with my glue stick? I'd better borrow Arthur's."

Luckily Arthur was downstairs so didn't see me sneaking into his room this time.

I got to work, cutting and sticking. Soon there was glitter everywhere! When I'd finished, I did a twirl in front of the mirror and pretended to wave a wand.

"What do you think, Hammy? Pretty good, eh?"

They were great wings. Even if they *were* a bit lopsided. And one of them kept falling off on to the floor. And they both dripped glitter every time I moved. Still, I could pretend the glitter was fairy dust.

I did another twirl – and trod on Arthur's glue stick and squashed it into the rug.

Oops!

I thought I might go and show Mum my wings. But then I remembered she was trying to sleep and I had a better idea.

"I know what fairy godmothers do," I told Hammy. "Good deeds! And now I've got my wings, I can feel a good deed coming on right now."

I went tripping downstairs, where Arthur was giving his pet rat, Haggis, rides on his skateboard in the hall. "That looks fun," I said. "Maybe Hammy could have a go later."

"Why have you got bits of cardboard

stuck on your back?" Arthur asked.

I ignored him. Some people just don't have enough magic in them to know a pair of fairy wings when they see them.

I went through to the kitchen, where my dad was fixing tea.

"Hi, Chloe," he said, without looking round. "Don't make too much noise – your mum has one of her migraines."

"I won't," I promised.

I walked past him to the fridge and reached into the freezer compartment. Dad was too busy chopping onions to notice me. I fetched what I needed and tiptoed back upstairs and into Mum's bedroom.

Mum had her eyes shut and she looked flushed and hot. Poor Mum! What a brilliant idea of mine to bring her some ice! It was just the thing to help her aching head.

Lucky Mum, to have a kind, thoughtful daughter like me.

I held the ice-cube tray upside down over Mum. Then very gently, so as not to wake her, I tapped it. Not a single ice cube came out. I tapped harder. Still nothing. So then I thumped the back of the tray.

KERPLUNK!

All the ice cubes fell out – right on to Mum, who gave a screech.

"Oof! What's happening?"

"I've brought some ice to cool your poor hot head," I explained.

Mum spluttered and glared at me. She was really mad!

I could see that doing good deeds was going to be harder than I had thought.

Chapter Four

On Wednesday afternoon, Eliza's dad picked us up from school and we all went back to Eliza's house for the first meeting of the Secret Fairy Godmother Club.

The things I like about Eliza's house are:

♥ Hercules, Eliza's French bulldog. He's really sweet.

♥ There's a huge garden to play in.

♥ *There are no pesky brothers rushing around and getting in our way.*

The things I don't like are:
♥ *The food. Eliza's mum is very into healthy eating. Even Hercules eats vegetarian dog food.*
♥ *There are lots of expensive gadgets, and I'm always nervous about breaking them. (Sometimes I have broken them.)*
♥ *Too many stairs.*

Today, Eliza's mum was waiting for us in the kitchen, and the first thing she said was, "Hello, girls! Look at the lovely carrot sticks I've got ready for you!" When we were munching our healthy carrots and sipping our healthy tap water, she said, "Has Eliza told you our wonderful news?"

We said yes. Actually, Aisha and I had

33

been sneaking secret looks at her bump whenever we thought she wasn't looking. It was already quite big!

"Eliza is very excited about the baby," she told Aisha and me.

"No, I'm not," growled Eliza.

Her mum gave a tinkly laugh. "You are funny, sweetie," she said, and left the room.

"She's in a good mood, isn't she?" I said.

Eliza just growled again. She sounded like Hercules does when you step too close to his bone.

We started up the stairs to Eliza's bedroom. There are a *lot* of stairs, because Eliza's room is in the attic. Halfway up we stopped for a rest.

"That was going to be my den," said Eliza, pointing across the landing. "Mum and Dad *promised*."

Aisha and I peeped inside. It was a little

room, all bare and empty.

"Didn't this used to be your mum's office?" asked Aisha.

"Yes, but she's having one built in the garden instead. She said I could have this for my very own special den. Only now the baby's getting it!"

Aisha and I exchanged looks. Eliza has a gorgeous bedroom of her own. It's much bigger than either of ours. She didn't really need another room too. But we could see it wasn't the best time to say so.

"I wouldn't want this room if I were you," I said firmly. "I mean, there's no furniture. And the walls and carpet are really boring."

"Good," said Eliza. "I don't want the baby to have a nice room."

"It could be lovely, though," said Aisha thoughtfully. "Imagine if there were animal pictures on the walls. We could paint some ourselves … and find a rug."

"And a crib!" I burst out. "With curtains and a mobile hanging over the top!"

"You could bring down some of your cuddly toys," Aisha said to Eliza.

Eliza made a face. "Hmm. I guess I do have a lot of toys. And it would be fun decorating this room. So I suppose the baby could have a few – not my best ones though," she added. "Definitely not Mr Mouse."

"Let's do it, then," said Aisha. "It can be a wonderful surprise for when the baby is born! We'll gather all the bits. It can be one of our Fairy Godmother Tasks."

We went upstairs, still chattering about our idea. When we reached Eliza's room, all of us (including Hercules) sat in a circle on Eliza's purple stripy cushions, and Eliza offered all of us (including Hercules) a wafer biscuit from her secret store.

"I think Hercules thinks he's a fairy godmother too," Aisha said, grinning.

Then Eliza announced, "I call the first meeting of the Secret Fairy Godmother Club to order!"

Aisha fetched a brand new notebook out of her pocket. "I thought we had better have a new one now we are being fairy godmothers," she explained. On the front was a beautiful butterfly with wings that looked just like a fairy's.

"And I've got badges," she went on. Aisha is brilliant at making things. Our badges had an A, a C and an E written on them in curly writing, and a little magic wand next to them.

"A for Araminta, C for Clarinda and E for Elisabetta," I said, as we pinned them

to our T-shirts. "Those were our princess names."

"They're just as good for fairy godmothers," said Eliza happily.

Aisha has the best handwriting, so always makes notes for our club. She wrote carefully on the first page of the notebook.

Fairy Godmother Tasks
1. Decorate the baby's bedroom.

Then she looked up. "What else shall we do? Maybe we could make gifts for when it's born?"

Eliza pouted a bit. "I don't think *everything* should be about the baby."

I said, "One thing fairy godmothers do is good deeds. Maybe we could help people – you know, by making their dreams come true."

"My dream is not having a baby brother or sister," Eliza said, but Aisha and I ignored her.

"It's a good idea, Chloe," said Aisha. "I wonder what kind of good deeds fairy godmothers do?" Before we could answer she beamed and went on. "I know –

they help people find true love. Like in *Cinderella*."

"True love!" said Eliza. "That's soppy. I want to do a spell!"

"No, true love," Aisha insisted. "Like the fairy godmother in *Cinderella*, who helped her find Prince Charming!"

That was when I had my wonderful idea. "I know! We can do both. Spells and true love! Our very first good deed will be making a magical love potion!"

I was really pleased with myself because not only had I managed to use both Aisha and Eliza's suggestions, I loved the idea of making a potion!

Aisha and Eliza loved the idea too.

"Brilliant!" Aisha exclaimed. "There's just one thing—"

Eliza chimed in. "How *do* you make a love potion?"

Fairy Godmother Tasks
1. Decorate the baby's bedroom.
2. Make a magical love potion.

Chapter Five

When I got home I rushed to look in Mum and Dad's cookbooks to see if I could find a recipe for a love potion. I found recipes for smoothies and soups and salads and stews – but no love potions. Eliza and Aisha didn't have any luck either.

So then we thought we would look at some fairy tales.

"Maybe Cinderella's fairy godmother

used a potion," said Aisha hopefully. "Let's look and see."

There are five different books about Cinderella in our school library. Five! During library time, we read every one. But none of them explained how the fairy godmother did her magic. She just waved her wand – and hey, presto, the pumpkin turned into a carriage, and Cinderella was off to the ball!

"Maybe Cinderella and Prince Charming fell in love by themselves," Aisha whispered, as she turned the pages. "The fairy godmother just magicked the pumpkin into a coach and the mice into horses."

"Well, I wouldn't mind doing that kind of magic," I said. "But it still doesn't say *how*."

"Who are we going to give this love potion to, anyway?" Eliza asked. "I mean there's no point making it if we don't know who it's *for*."

"That's true." Aisha looked worried.

"Don't worry," I told them. "I know exactly who it's for."

"Who?"

"Hammy."

"But who are you going to make him fall in love with?" Eliza asked.

"Another hamster, of course. Lots of people have pet hamsters so I'm sure we can find one. But hamsters are quite shy, so when I *have* found a girl hamster, I think it will help if they can have a sip of love potion."

Eliza and Aisha really liked this idea.

"Maybe they could have a hamster wedding," suggested Aisha, her eyes shining. "We could make them little wedding outfits and everything."

"And then they'll have lots of little hamster babies," I finished happily.

"You know what," said Eliza, shutting her book with a thud. "We don't need a recipe. We'll invent one ourselves."

We were so excited we'd forgotten to whisper. And we hadn't noticed Mr Carter coming up behind us.

"There seems to be rather a lot of chatting going on over here," he remarked. "And what are you reading? You're supposed to be doing research for our wildlife project. *Those* don't look like wildlife books to me." He pointed to a picture of Cinderella before she goes to the ball.

"Mice are wildlife," suggested Eliza hopefully, showing him the mice who were about to be turned into footmen.

"Hmm," said Mr Carter. "We'll be lucky

to see mice on our nature walk, with all you children running around."

"What nature walk?" Aisha asked.

Mr Carter groaned and rolled his eyes. He looked so funny that we all laughed. "Does anyone ever listen to me?" he wondered aloud. "If you three *had* been paying attention, you'd have heard me say that we are going on a class nature walk next week, in Thoresby Woods. You are supposed to be looking up some of the plants, insects and other wildlife we might find there."

He pushed some books towards us. "Now, how about doing a bit of work? Or I might just reconsider why it is I let you three sit together!"

He went off to sort out Barney, Mikhail and Arthur, who were pretending to be bats. At least, I think they were. There was lots of squeaking, anyway. And Barney seemed to be trying to fly.

Reluctantly, we picked up the wildlife books.

Aisha started reading a book called *Insects*. Eliza was reading *Woodland Animals*. I was left with *Plants of the Hedgerow*. It wasn't very exciting. Just lots of pictures of leaves and long plant names.

Then, to my surprise, I started getting interested. "Do you know what it says here?" I whispered to Aisha and Eliza. "It says that people often used plants to make medicines and other potions. They thought they could cure diseases. And they even believed they had magical properties! Maybe that's what we need for our love potion."

Aisha and Eliza were excited too. They stopped looking at *Insects* and *Woodland*

Animals and came and peered over my shoulders instead.

I turned a few more pages. Suddenly I sat bolt upright, "Hey! Look ... this is a picture of a wild rose."

"So?" said Eliza.

"Well, it says here that many people consider it to be the flower of true love! We should definitely include that in our love potion!"

"Oooh!" Eliza leaned closer.

"A wild rose!" Aisha clasped her hands. "That sounds like something straight out of a fairy tale!"

We grinned at each other. Our love potion was going to happen after all! We linked little fingers under the table and did our special Secret Club Finger Shake. Up-down-up!

"What are you lot doing?" It was Barney.

He was sticking his nose in where it wasn't wanted, as usual. He looked at the book, puzzled. "Why are you getting all excited about boring old plants?"

I smiled mysteriously. "Wouldn't *you* like to know?"

We wanted to start plant-gathering straight away, but first we had to persuade someone to take us. It wasn't as easy as you'd think.

"I thought you liked country walks!" I complained to my mum.

"I do, Chloe," Mum replied. "But I'm busy this week. I can't drop everything to take you and Aisha and Eliza flower-picking!"

"I thought you said healthy exercise was way better than watching TV," I said to my dad.

49

"I know. But there's golf on the telly," said Dad sheepishly.

Eliza tried to get her parents to take us out with Hercules. But her mum was feeling too tired for long walks, and her dad liked to go jogging and he didn't think we'd keep up.

In the end, Aisha's dad, Mr Akbal, took us down to the playground with her little brothers. While he was keeping an eye on Hari, Abdullah and Ibrahim, we went hunting about in the overgrown bits. There were loads of plants growing there. We filled a whole carrier bag.

After we got back to Aisha's house we went straight to Aisha's room, and shoved a chair against the door so her brothers couldn't interrupt us. Eliza emptied the bag on to the floor. There were:

♥ *Dandelions*

♥ *Grass*

♥ *Clover leaves*

♥ *Something extremely prickly (ouch!)*

♥ *A crisp packet*

♥ *A white pebble*

"Why the crisp packet?" I asked.

"Oh, I picked that up," said Aisha. "I thought fairy godmothers should help clear up the litter." She put the crisp packet in the bin.

"And the pebble's mine," said Eliza. "I collect them." And she stuck it in her pocket. "What about this plant – ouch!"

I sucked my finger.

"I think that's a thistle," Aisha said helpfully. "You can tell from the spiky leaves."

"Well, we're not putting *that* in. It would taste all prickly. Still, Hammy will love these dandelion leaves. They're his favourite."

"I've heard that clover is good for hamsters, too," said Eliza.

"OK." Aisha moved the chair and peered around the bedroom door. "The boys are watching a DVD. I can hear *Thomas the Tank Engine*. I reckon the kitchen is clear!"

We gathered our ingredients and made for the stairs. It was time to make a love potion!

Chapter Six

We spread everything out on the kitchen counter.

Aisha's mum makes a lot of curries and she often grinds her own spices in a big pestle and mortar. We used it to pound away at all the stuff we'd gathered. Slowly it turned into a thick, gloopy paste.

"This is great," said Eliza, pounding fiercely. "I'm imagining this is all the people I don't like … like Mum and Dad."

Aisha and I exchanged looks. Obviously Eliza hadn't forgiven her parents yet.

"It's meant to be a *love* potion," I pointed out. "You should be thinking about things you *love*. Otherwise you might spoil the magic."

"Oh, all right ... I'll think about Hercules." Eliza pounded more slowly. "I don't know. I feel bad now, like maybe I'm squashing his tail."

"You don't have to *imagine* anyone," said Aisha firmly, taking the pestle. "You should just think lovely thoughts instead." She began to chant.

"Roses are red,
Violets are blue,
Sugar is sweet
And so are you!"

It sounded good, like a spell.

"It's not going red or blue, though," Eliza said. "And it doesn't smell sweet either."

"Then let's add a few more things," I said.

We rummaged around the kitchen cupboards. While we were doing it, Aisha's mum came in. To my surprise she didn't pay us any attention. She just went and sat at the table and opened her laptop. "Don't mind me," she murmured, as she began tapping at the keys.

We found some good things for our potion:

Honey. ("Everyone knows nothing is sweeter than honey!" said Eliza.)

Rosewater Syrup. ("That sounds like the sort of the thing that should definitely be in a fairy godmother spell," I said.)

Cardamom. ("It's my favourite spice," Aisha explained as she sprinkled it on.)

We were sieving our potion when Hari,
Ibrahim and Abdullah ran into the room.

"Puffa, puffa, puffa, puffa, puffa!" they
yelled, and Hari crashed into the table.

"Oh my goodness," said Aisha's mum,
grabbing her laptop out of harm's way.
"Their DVD must have finished. And I
really need to get this done. Aisha, could
you do me a favour and put the TV on?"

Aisha went out. Her little brothers

followed, shouting, "More Thomas!" and "No, I want Peppa Pig!" and "No, Mr Tumble!" at the very tops of their voices.

Mrs Akbal blinked and looked at us, as if she had noticed us for the first time. "What are you girls up to? Is it something for school?"

Eliza and I looked at each other. "It's a kind of experiment," said Eliza. (Which was true.)

"And we're going to clear up, I promise," I added, looking around at the mess we had made. There were leaves and twigs everywhere and a long green smear down the front of the kitchen cupboards. The Akbal house is always very tidy.

"Don't worry about it," said Mrs Akbal, staring at her laptop.

"What are *you* doing?" I asked rather shyly. Mrs Akbal was usually bustling around the house, cooking and cleaning and trying to stop the boys from destroying everything.

"It's a course I'm doing," Mrs Akbal explained. "It's interesting, but it's hard to concentrate when the boys are around."

Aisha had come back into the room. "Can I tell them, Mum?" she asked. Mrs Akbal nodded. "Mum and Dad are starting their very own business," Aisha said proudly. "That's why Mum needs to learn all kinds of things to help run it, like she's doing now. And Dad's doing the driving. But he's not going to drive a taxi any more. It's going to be a business that does fancy cars for things like weddings."

"Ooh!" we said.

"Maybe he'll take you for rides!" said Eliza. "Think what all the other kids will say if you arrive at school in a limousine!"

Aisha giggled. "Maybe we can all ride together!"

I had an idea. "We can make a special good-luck charm for the business!"

Aisha and Eliza frowned at me. But Mrs Akbal wasn't listening to us. She had already bent over her laptop again.

"You almost gave it all away," hissed Eliza.

"Yes, you have to pay attention," Aisha agreed.

I blushed. "I don't think she noticed. Anyway, it was a good idea."

"Let's finish the love potion first, shall we?" Eliza suggested.

We poured it carefully into a jar. Then we all looked at it.

Eliza said, "It doesn't look very…"

"…nice," I admitted.

"It's the *colour*," said Aisha. "It looks like seaweed."

"And the *smell*," said Eliza. "It reminds me of Hercules, that time he jumped in a muddy pond."

"Still," Aisha said, "just because it looks bad and smells bad, that doesn't mean it won't work."

"It won't work if nobody will drink it," said Eliza. "And who wants to drink pongy old pondwater?"

We stood silently for a moment. Then I thought of something. "I know what the problem is!"

"What?" asked Eliza.

"Yes, tell us, Clarinda," said Aisha.

"Well, that book said we needed a *wild rose*. It's wild roses that are to do with love, remember?"

"Of course," said Eliza slowly.

Aisha gave an excited squeak.

"I wish you wouldn't do that right next

61

to my ear," I said.

"But I've just thought! When we go on the school nature walk – we can look for a wild rose then. Surely we can find one in those huge great woods?"

I looked at her admiringly. "You are clever, Araminta!"

"Yes, that's brilliant," Eliza agreed.

We could hardly wait for our trip to the woods!

Chapter Seven

At ten o'clock on Wednesday we all gathered at the school gates, waiting to set off on the nature walk.

There were loads of us, because Mrs Wheaton's class was coming too. The playground was full of kids milling around, trying to decide who they wanted to walk with, dropping their lunch boxes on each other's feet or discovering they had forgotten their water bottle and then going up to the nearest grown-up and saying, "Please, can I go and fetch it?" Meanwhile Mr Carter and Mrs Wheaton were trying to count us all and going crazy because everyone kept moving about.

In all the excitement, nobody was paying attention to Aisha, Eliza and me, so we were able to make our plans.

"We must stick together in the woods," said Eliza importantly.

"Yes, and we need to get away from everyone else so that they don't see what we're doing," I agreed.

"Especially people like Rachel," said Aisha, "who like to interfere."

"Or Barney and Arthur," I added. "It would be terrible if they found out about our club! They'd tell everybody."

We checked over the stuff we'd brought with us.

Eliza had a clean plastic bag to put the wild rose in (if we found one). And a picture from the internet of exactly what a wild rose looked like.

I'd brought a magnifying glass to look at plants through. (It actually belonged to Arthur and I was hoping he wouldn't notice I'd taken it.) I'd also sneaked a pair of my mum's gardening gloves. (I was hoping she wouldn't notice they'd gone either!)

Aisha had brought the jar of potion and a spoon to stir it with.

"Do you think we should have brought the potion?" Eliza asked. "What if Mr Carter sees it?"

"I don't think it's safe to leave at home," Aisha explained. "My mum might throw it out."

"Also, if we can add the wild rose right

away, while it's fresh, then that will help the magic," I suggested.

While we'd been chatting, Mr Carter had been getting more and more impatient. "Right!" he barked suddenly. "Everyone is to stand still as a statue. Barney, that includes you! And if that is your lunch you've been eating, you're going to be very hungry later."

Barney's cheeks were puffed out like Hammy's, they were so full of food. He tried to swallow it all at once and began to choke. Arthur banged him on the back.

"Mr Carter, he's choking to death!" yelled Mikhail.

"Emergency! Emergency!" shrieked Keira.

"I've done a first-aid course," announced Rachel. "Let me through!"

With that, a chunk of food shot out

of Barney's mouth and hit Keira on the nose. (She wasn't pleased.) Mr Carter told everyone to calm down. He wasn't looking very calm himself. All his hair was standing up on end.

"Now I've had enough nonsense. We're never going to get going at this rate. This is a final warning. If I hear the slightest peep out of anyone—"

"Mr Carter," said someone behind him.

Mr Carter's face went very red. Then he exploded!

"RIGHT! THAT'S IT! WHICHEVER SILLY PERSON SAID THAT, I AM SENDING YOU STRAIGHT BACK TO SCHOOL!"

He turned to see who it was that had interrupted him and there stood ... Mrs Khan, our head teacher. She was all dressed for hiking in the woods.

Everyone began to giggle. Mr Carter looked really embarrassed.

"Oh, Mrs Khan! I didn't mean *you*!"

Finally, everyone began to settle down. We all got into line. Aisha, Eliza and I were planning to walk together, but when Mrs Khan saw this she wasn't pleased.

"You're supposed to be walking in pairs, girls."

"Oh, Mr Carter always lets us walk together," I said quickly. "You see, we're special friends, and Mr Carter says he can trust us to behave and—"

But Mrs Khan took no notice. "Rachel seems to be part of a three too," she said briskly. "So I think the best thing is if Eliza and Rachel pair up. And I don't want to hear any arguments," she added.

We fairy godmothers looked at each other in dismay. We didn't want to walk with

69

Rachel! We couldn't talk about magic and potions with her there. And we definitely didn't want to risk her finding out about our club.

But there was nothing we could do. Rachel moved up next to Eliza and we set off through the school gates.

The three of us were very quiet as we walked past the bus stop and down the hill that leads past the library. Rachel didn't seem to notice, though. She was too busy telling us all about the wildlife she planned to see in the woods. She went on and on about the different kinds of animals as if she was some kind of world expert. "Of course what I'd really love to see is an owl," she said at last. "I expect you didn't know there are lots of different kinds of owl, did you? Tawny owls, snowy owls, barn owls. But they are all very rare."

"I saw an owl one night from my window," Eliza commented.

"I don't believe you," said Rachel at once. She smiled at Eliza in her most annoying manner.

Eliza flushed. "I did so!"

Rachel raised her eyebrows. "I think you're being a bit silly, aren't you, Eliza? I mean, nobody sees an owl out of their window."

I could tell Eliza was furious. Aisha and me were too. How dare Rachel say our friend was lying?

"Eliza's telling the truth," I said, turning round to look at Rachel. "She's not being silly at all."

"No," Aisha agreed. "And her room is in the attic. Of course she could see an owl from up there."

Eliza smiled gratefully at us. "I saw it

71

through the skylight," she said. "It had a mouse in its beak."

Rachel was cross. She doesn't like it when people don't agree with her. "You're making it up. Since you started being friends with Chloe, you're becoming just like her. You don't know what's real and what isn't."

"That's not true!" Eliza was looking so mad I was afraid she was about to start doing her karate. I wasn't pleased with Rachel either.

Before we could all get into a big fight, Aisha interrupted. "Ooh, look!" she said. "Isn't that a lovely dress?"

We were passing a row of shops, and Aisha was pointing at a wedding dress

in one of the windows.

Eliza loves pretty clothes. She forgot all about owls and Rachel. "Ooh!" she said. "It's beautiful."

"Just like Cinderella," I agreed.

"It's not bad," said Rachel coolly. "But it's not as nice as my auntie's. *Her* dress is much nicer."

"Is your auntie getting married, then?" asked Aisha.

"Yes, and I'm being her bridesmaid. The *chief* bridesmaid," added Rachel. "Everyone will be relying on me."

I think we were all getting fed up with Rachel by then, especially Eliza. "I've *always* wanted to be a bridesmaid," she hissed at me, as we crossed the road and Rachel went ahead. "And nobody ever asks me! I *hate* that Rachel."

"I was a bridesmaid once," I said

comfortingly. "It wasn't that great. My dress was too tight because I grew too much before the wedding. And then I stood on the bride's dress and it ripped … luckily my Auntie Jackie saw the funny side."

Aisha gripped my arm. "Look, are those the woods?"

We forgot about bridesmaids and peered at the line of trees ahead.

"I think so!" My heart leaped and my imagination began to race.

Woods are such magical places! Fairies live in woods … and come out at midnight to dance around toadstools. Hansel and Gretel got lost in the woods and ended up at a witch's cottage. Little Red Riding Hood was followed by a wolf through the wood. Sleeping Beauty was surrounded by woods that grew up after she fell asleep for a hundred years. The prince had to fight his way through thorns and thickets while the good fairy godmothers helped him on his way.

I just couldn't keep my thoughts to myself. The words came tumbling out as I grabbed Aisha and Eliza's hands. (Rachel was chatting to Keira and Georgia so she didn't overhear.)

"Do you think this could be a magic wood? I think it is, don't you? We'd better keep an eye out for the Big Bad Wolf ... and keep together in case we have to fight off a wicked witch ... and look out for woodcutters and gingerbread cottages!"

Aisha and Eliza's eyes grew round and bright with excitement.

"Ooh, I can't wait!" Aisha whispered.

"I'm sure we're going to have the most wonderful adventure!" Eliza declared.

And with that we went skipping into the woods, hand in hand.

Chapter Eight

I felt the springy moss under my feet as I walked. Above me, birds twittered and cooed in the branches. A squirrel went racing along a branch and leaped into a nearby tree.

In the distance we could hear other kids from school moving through the undergrowth or shouting to each other when they found something interesting. Rachel had gone to join her friends. Mr Carter had told us to come at once if we heard his whistle, but we didn't have to walk all together any more.

I led the way down a winding path.

At first we were excited by every acorn and every pebble. But after we'd calmed down (and realized we weren't going to come across a fairy around every corner) we remembered we were searching for a wild rose. So we began to look at every plant we saw. We found ferns, grasses, blackberries, nettles, toadstools, wild garlic and moss. As Eliza said, it was amazing how many plants *weren't* wild roses.

Then I gave a squeak of excitement.

"Look, I can see red ... through these leaves ... under these bushes ... it's a rose, it must be ... *it is* ... how *wonderful* ... oh, no, it's just a Coke can."

"Never mind," said Aisha cheerfully. "I'm sure we'll find one soon."

We didn't, though. Before long we were

feeling less like three fairy godmothers on a quest for a magical wild rose and more like three cross girls who were getting tired and hot.

"My feet hurt!" I said.

"My arms are all scratched," said Aisha.

"I'm hungry!" said Eliza. "I'm going to die of starvation if I don't eat something!"

"It'll be time for lunch soon," Aisha pointed out.

Eliza cheered up. "Ooh, yes! And guess what I've got? Someone at Mum's work gave her cupcakes at her baby shower, and Mum said I could take one as a special treat. It's got vanilla icing and it's one of those scrummy yummy ones that looks like it has butterfly wings on top."

"So there are some good things about the baby coming," I pointed out.

"I suppose so," Eliza admitted. She picked

up her lunch bag. "I might have a nibble now."

"You mustn't – Mr Carter said we had to wait," Aisha objected.

"Besides, we can't give up on the potion," I said. "How about we pretend these sticks are wands?" I picked up a long one and waved it in the air. "Then they can draw us towards the rose …
I can almost feel the wand pulling me now…"

Aisha and Eliza watched as I stood on one leg, waving my wand. I was sure its magic would lead me in the right direction.

"Oh, wand, take me to the fairy glade!" I declared. "And there let me find a wild rose!"

I waited. And waited. But that wand

wasn't leading me anywhere.

"Maybe there *aren't* any wild roses," said Eliza. "Maybe it's the wrong time of year."

"No! There must be a wild rose … there *must*!"

"Let's have some cake," Eliza suggested.

Aisha pointed at a branch. "What's that bird? I've never seen one like that before."

Despite my disappointment, I was interested. The bird had a red cap and it was pecking at the tree.

TAP! TAP! TAP!

"I think it's a woodpecker," I said. "I've never seen one either."

"That will show Rachel," said Eliza. "She thinks she knows everything about wildlife, but I bet she's never seen a woodpecker."

I took a step towards the bird.

"Careful, you'll frighten it!" said Aisha, as it flew to another tree.

"No, I won't." I crept after it, trying not to make a sound. It was strange, but I almost felt like it *wanted* me to follow it. I was very close, when suddenly it flew high into the air and away. I sighed, and was about to go back to the others when...

"Look at this!" I yelled.

"What is it?"

"Come and see!"

Eliza and Aisha came running. I pointed. There, growing under the very same tree that the bird had been sitting in, was a wild rose. We could hardly believe it.

"It must have been a *magic* woodpecker," Aisha whispered. I nodded.

Carefully, we picked the rose, then Aisha unscrewed the lid of the jar and we added some of the petals to our potion. Eliza found a small twig and stirred, while we all recited the same lines:

"Roses are red
Violets are blue
Sugar is sweet
And so are you!"

"Do you think it matters that the rose is white, not red?" I wondered, but Eliza and Aisha said they were sure it would be fine. We set off again through the trees, feeling very pleased with ourselves. We had completed one of our Fairy Godmother Tasks! Now I couldn't wait to try out the love potion. Lucky Hammy! I could just picture him running around his exercise wheel, with his own true love running beside him.

I was all wrapped up in my lovely dream ... until I came down to earth with a thud. I was being pelted with dead leaves while three horrible monsters were shrieking and howling as they came leaping out at us from behind the trees!

Chapter Nine

After a few seconds I realized they weren't monsters. Or not exactly. They were Arthur, Mikhail and Barney. They were covered in leaves and moss, which is why I hadn't recognized them at first.

"Gotcha!" yelled Arthur, sticking a pine cone down the back of my shirt.

"Poopy girls!" shouted Barney, pelting Aisha with moss.

"You can't catch us!" shrieked Mikhail.

"We'll see about that!" I yelled. I grabbed some dead leaves off the ground ready to hurl at them. Aisha bent down and started gathering pine cones.

As for Eliza, she went straight into karate mode.

"Hai cha!"

She launched herself through the air. Her arms were going round like windmills.

The boys took one look at her and ran for their lives! The only thing was, she had forgotten she was still carrying her lunch bag. It fell out of her hands ... and the beautiful, special, scrummy yummy cupcake went flying out of the bag and through the air. It landed *SPLASH* in the middle of a stream.

Oops.

"Just think," said Aisha comfortingly to Eliza, as we were sat eating our lunches half an hour later, "if there *are* fairies in the wood then maybe they will use your cupcake as a boat. That's exactly what it looked like, floating away on the water."

"Yes," I agreed. "I can just imagine them climbing aboard and sitting on the cupcake with their little toes dangling in the stream ... and if they get hungry they can break off a piece as a treat."

Eliza chewed moodily on her houmous sandwich. "It was *my* cupcake. I was looking forward to it."

"Surely you wouldn't mind giving your cake to a real live fairy?"

"Yes, I *would*."

"Have a samosa," said Aisha kindly. "My mum made them."

Around us, the rest of our class were munching their lunches and boasting about the things they'd seen. After a while, Mr Carter glanced at his watch and told us all to get a move on. Some of the boys had finished eating and started messing about, so he gave them a big bin bag and told them to gather up the rubbish.

"Any litter?" asked Barney, waving the bin bag under our noses. He grinned at Eliza. "I saw your cupcake go into the stream, Eliza. I bet there's a duck eating it this very minute. I bet he's really enjoying it. Quack, quack!" He jumped up and down pretending to be a duck.

"Well, you didn't get any lunch at all," I pointed out, as Eliza glowered at him. "You'd already eaten yours in the playground."

"I did so," said Barney. "I told Mr Carter I would starve to death, and he gave me some of his. I had half a cheese roll *and* some crisps *and* some chocolate brownie!"

"That's so unfair," Eliza grumbled.

"He let me have his apple juice too!" He waved the bottle at Eliza but that was a mistake. She grabbed it off him. Barney tried to get it back, but Eliza wouldn't let go so he yelled, "I didn't want any more anyhow!" and ran off into the trees.

Eliza was furious.

"Why should Barney get chocolate

brownie when I lost my special cupcake?"

"It's not very fair," I agreed. "How about I bake you some more cupcakes to make up for it?"

Eliza wasn't listening. "Pass me the potion!"

"Why?" I asked rather nervously. I didn't like the glint in Eliza's eye.

"Because I'm going to give Barney some. Only I'm going to add lots of slugs and beetles first!"

Aisha and I stared at each other in horror.

"Fairy godmothers don't do things like that," I protested.

"And it's not very fair on the slugs and beetles," Aisha pointed out.

"I don't care."

"But, Eliza," Aisha said. "Fairy godmothers are supposed to do good deeds and make people happy!"

"This will make *me* happy!" Eliza said. And she poured some potion into the bottle of apple juice. "Ha, ha!" she cackled. "He'll think it's just apple juice that I'm giving him."

Aisha and me looked at each other. "I think Eliza has decided to be a *bad* fairy," Aisha whispered. "Like the one that sent Sleeping Beauty to sleep for a hundred years!"

I nodded. Aisha was right. But what could we do?

"Maybe Barney won't drink it," I whispered. "It doesn't look very nice."

Eliza heard me. "Oh, yes he will," she said. "He's greedy, that's why. Now I'm going to find a slug."

"No!" I said sternly. "I'm not going to let you!"

"Me neither," said Aisha firmly. "And if

you do, then you can't be a fairy godmother any more."

Eliza hesitated. None of us noticed Mr Carter coming up behind us.

"Everyone is *supposed* to have finished their lunch," he said briskly, making us jump. "Eliza, put your things away."

Before Eliza could say anything, Mr Carter caught sight of the plastic bottle. "Hey! That looks like my apple juice! Where did you get that?"

"Barney left it," said Eliza quickly. "Don't worry. I'll put it in the litter bag."

"No need," said Mr Carter. "I'm still thirsty. I'll drink it."

Before anybody could say a word he grabbed the bottle.

Eliza, Aisha and I stared at him in horror as he put it to his mouth and took a huge swig of potion!

I couldn't take my eyes off him. Had we *poisoned* Mr Carter? Or (almost as bad) was he about to fall in love with someone? Were Eliza and Aisha and I going to be in terrible trouble? Was our secret going to be discovered?

The next moment Mr Carter made a face then spat out the potion over the grass.

"Ugh!" he said.

Surely we'd be in terrible trouble now!

"It's not her fault!" I squeaked. "Eliza couldn't help wanting to be a bad fairy. Aisha and I should have

stopped her, and besides, she wouldn't have been a bad fairy only she's been a bit upset lately, what with babies and Barney and her

92

cupcake falling in the stream, even if it did get to be a fairy boat and – anyway, all I mean is, *please* don't be cross, Mr Carter! Even if you have got a bad tummy!"

"Really, Chloe, calm down," Mr Carter said. "I can't understand a word you're saying." He emptied the rest of the bottle on to the grass. "No wonder Barney left that apple juice – it's obviously gone off."

And he went striding off to help Mrs Khan who was rolling up the picnic rugs.

We three fairy godmothers looked at each other.

Phew!

Fairy Godmother Tasks
1. Decorate the baby's bedroom.
2. Make a magical love potion. ✓
3. Find a wild rose. ✓

Chapter Ten

The next meeting of the Secret Fairy Godmother Club was at my house. As a special treat for Eliza, I made us all cupcakes and arranged them on a pink-and-white plate.

"Ooh, thank you, Chloe!" Eliza picked up a cupcake and looked at it. "Err, it's a bit of a funny shape."

"Yes, more like a saucer than a cup," Aisha agreed.

"I know," I
apologized. "I'm not
sure what went wrong.
I think it's because I
was imagining I was
a cook in the palace
kitchens, making cakes
for Cinderella's ball,

and so I forgot to count the eggs I was
putting in the bowl. And you can't really get
them out once you've added them…"

"It still tastes good," said Eliza, with her
mouth full.

"Let's write down what we've been
doing," said Aisha, opening the special club
notebook.

"We've been quite busy, really," I said.

It was true. For one thing, we had
made fairy godmother costumes. My old
cardboard wings hadn't lasted very long

95

(wearing them in the bath had definitely been a mistake) but Aisha, who is really good at crafts, had shown us how to make some more out of net stretched over gold wire. They really did look fantastic!

"Anyone would think I was a real fairy!" I said, putting them on and wriggling my shoulders to make them flap.

"Watch it, Chloe – you almost bopped me with them," said Eliza. "What else have we done?"

"Well, Aisha's mum and dad really liked the good-luck charm we made for their new business."

That was true. We'd made the charm out of lucky white heather and tied a gold ribbon round it, and Aisha's dad had hung it up in the windscreen of the fancy vintage car he had bought. He hadn't been so keen on the fairy dust we'd scattered, though.

Apparently he'd just washed the car and wasn't pleased to have glitter all over the bonnet.

We were also dying to give somebody a makeover (just like the fairy godmother did with Cinderella) but so far the only somebody we'd found to do one on was Hercules. And when we tried to squeeze him into Aisha's doll's jacket and tie a ribbon to his tail, he'd wriggled and run away.

"What about the baby's bedroom?" asked Aisha. "Can we come round soon and decorate it?"

"I hope so. But Mum's been too tired for me to have friends round. It's the baby's fault," Eliza added. "It keeps kicking her. It wakes her up at night."

"Maybe it's going to like karate, like you," Aisha suggested.

"Yes, you can teach it when it gets bigger," I added.

Eliza liked this idea. "Yes, maybe," she agreed. "I've tried teaching Hercules but dog's legs don't bend right … maybe a brother or sister would be different."

"Anyway, we're all collecting some lovely things," I said. "So when we do come to yours, Eliza, we can make the baby's room wonderful."

"Good." Aisha was looking at her list. "It's just a pity about the love potion. I guess we didn't put the lid on tight enough."

We sighed. When we got back to school, we'd discovered that the last of the potion had leaked all over Aisha's bag. "Yes, I really wanted it for Hammy," I said sadly. "I still want him to find his own true love."

"But Arthur told us you have to be really careful what you feed to hamsters," Eliza pointed out. "Plus, you don't even know another hamster for him to meet."

"I know. I've asked everyone. Next door and the postman and the lady at the corner shop and the window cleaner – it's amazing how many people don't have hamsters!"

"What *I* want is to send somebody to the ball, like Cinderella," Aisha interrupted. I think she was getting a bit bored of hearing about my search for Hammy's sweetheart. "They could travel in a horse and carriage. Actually I'd like to ride in a horse and carriage myself!"

Eliza and I looked at Aisha. Then we looked at each other. It was quite an idea.

I could just see it in my imagination – Aisha, Eliza and me, climbing into our carriage. A very handsome footman was holding the door open, while two beautiful white horses pawed at the ground. I was wearing a floaty blue dress, Eliza was wearing golden yellow, and Aisha was in red.

"I'd love it," I said.

"Shame it's impossible," said Eliza.

"*Why* is it impossible?" I asked.

"Well…" Eliza stared at me. "Where are we going to get a horse and carriage?"

I jumped up. "I know! We'll find one on the internet!"

I raced downstairs. Eliza and Aisha followed, Eliza still muttering that there was no way we would be able to find a horse and carriage. Mum's laptop was on the kitchen table and Mum was nowhere to be seen.

I started typing, and the next moment, there on the screen was…

Havelock's Horse and Carriage. Make Your Dream Come True!

I gazed at an image of a pair of dappled horses — almost as nice as the ones I'd imagined. A beautiful lady with long hair and a glittering gown was sitting in the carriage behind them, smiling and waving like anything.

"Beautiful!" whispered Aisha.

"Hmm," said Eliza.

I said, "It's not far away — just off the ring road."

"I think that's a bride and groom," said Eliza. "In that picture."

I peered at the screen. Now I looked closely, I could see the lady was wearing a white veil. And, yes – there *was* a man sitting there too. I hadn't noticed him before, dressed in his boring dark suit.

"Well, so what? It doesn't say *only* weddings, does it?"

"No," Aisha agreed. "It says 'Make Your Dream Come True'. And our dream is to ride in a horse and carriage."

"Well..." said Eliza doubtfully.

"I'm going to book it," I announced. And I started typing.

"Err, Chloe, are you *sure* this is a good idea?" asked Eliza.

"Yes," I said. "*Of course* I am. Don't you see? It's *meant* to be."

"Well..." said Eliza again.

"Done!" I announced grandly, as I pressed the button marked "Book Now".

"It says it costs five hundred pounds," said Eliza, reading over my shoulder.

I squeaked. "*What? Why didn't you stop me?*"

"I did try."

"But that's more than … more than … well, it's years and years of pocket money!" Aisha wailed.

We looked at each other. "We'll just have to tell them we've changed our minds," said Aisha at last. But when we read the website again, we couldn't find any way to send a message.

"Maybe I didn't book anything after all," I suggested.

We looked at each other doubtfully.

"I guess we'll just have to see what happens," said Aisha.

There didn't seem to be anything else we could do. Besides, at that moment Arthur came rushing into the kitchen.

"Look at my kite, Chloe!" he yelled. "I'm going to get Dad to take me to the park to try it out."

He waved his kite around. It had a long streamer tail and red and blue stickers all over it. It was a pretty good kite. It also looked … familiar.

"Did you make it yourself?" I asked.

"Nice colours," said Aisha. "I really like that dragon sticker."

"Yeah, I made it," said Arthur happily. "From something I found on the landing."

I gave a squeak. Then I felt my shoulders. Sure enough, one of them was bare.

"That's not a kite … that's one of my fairy wings!"

Chapter Eleven

The next day at school, we were all drawing the things we had seen on our nature walk.

I was concentrating on getting the petals of my wild rose just right, while half-listening to Barney and Rachel.

"What's that supposed to be?" Rachel asked Barney.

"A tree," Barney replied.

"Trees aren't purple."

"This one is," said Barney.

"And what about that orange thing?"

"It's a squirrel," Barney said.

"Squirrels have tails. That looks more like a hamster to me."

I put down my pen and looked at Barney's picture. There was an orange splodgy thing that *did* look a bit like a hamster. Except that if it *was* a hamster, then it was a giant hamster. I imagined a giant hamster bounding around Thoresby Woods and couldn't help giggling.

"How would you know?" said Barney. And he put his arm round his work so that Rachel couldn't see.

"I know all about hamsters," Rachel said, but Barney didn't reply.

"Have you got a hamster?" I asked Rachel.

"Yes. Emily."

"And Emily's a *girl* hamster?" I asked, just to be sure.

Rachel stared at me. "Well, I wouldn't call a boy Emily, would I?"

I was really excited. All this time I'd been trying to find people with girl hamsters, and here was Rachel, just across the table from me, who'd had one all along. Of course, Rachel wasn't my favourite person in the world, but I was prepared to overlook that for Hammy's sake.

I started telling her about how I was hoping to find a friend for my hamster. At first Rachel wasn't interested, but as I started talking about possible hamster weddings and cute little hamster babies, she changed her mind.

"Baby hamsters would be sweet," she admitted. "And so would a hamster wedding."

We talked a bit more, and decided that the best thing would be if I brought Hammy round to Rachel's house one day after school.

"I'll ask my mum to text your mum," said Rachel.

"All right," I agreed. "But don't let's tell our mums anything about the hamsters. I mean, you'd think anyone would love the idea of sweet little baby hamsters, but sometimes mums just don't see things the same way."

Rachel agreed.

I thought of something else.

"Can Eliza and Aisha come too?"

"Well…"

"Please. They won't want to be left out. You see—" I almost said, "We're all being fairy godmothers," but I managed not to.

"Oh, all right," said Rachel. "I'll ask Mum and see what she says."

*

Luckily, Rachel's mum said yes, and so a few days later we arrived at Rachel's house. I had brought Hammy with me in his special travel cage that he uses for going to the vet. Aisha and Eliza were there too, and Eliza had promised to be on her very best behaviour. "No being the Bad Fairy!" we'd told her.

Rachel's house is even bigger than Eliza's and even tidier than Aisha's. We had our snacks sitting on high stools at a breakfast bar in the kitchen. Then we went up to Rachel's room. It had wardrobes all down one side and it was very tidy too – even the pens and pencils on her desk were lined up, like soldiers on parade.

She led us to the corner of the room. "There's Emily," she said, pointing.

"Where?" I asked, peering into the cage. "*There!*"

At last I spotted a bit of golden fur. It

was Emily's ear. She was fast asleep, in a heap of hamster bedding.

Rachel didn't worry about that. She prodded Emily. "Wake up – we've got a friend for you to meet."

Eliza, Aisha and I got Hammy out of his box.

"Now you need a little sip of this, Hammy," said Aisha, unscrewing the lid of a small pink bottle.

"What's that?" Rachel demanded, staring at the pink liquid.

It was a new potion, but this time we'd just used ordinary water. (Aisha and Eliza had flat refused to go looking for any more wild roses!) We'd said our special "Roses are red" spell over it though, and I was sure it would help the hamsters to get off on the right foot.

We didn't want Rachel to know that we were making magic potions, though!

Aisha, Eliza and I looked at each other. "Umm – it's a very special Vitality Tonic," I invented quickly. "For hamsters. It's good for their fur. Emily can have some too."

"Well, OK, then," said Rachel. And she fetched Emily's water bottle.

The trouble was, after that nothing went to plan.

Firstly, the hamsters didn't like the love potion. They both refused to drink it.

Secondly, the hamsters didn't want to meet each other. For a long time they just sat and ignored each other.

Thirdly, when the hamsters finally said hello, they didn't take to each other. They gave one little snuffle. Then Emily biffed

Hammy with her paw. Hammy went to sulk in a corner and Emily went back to bed!

"I think it might be a while before we're organizing that hamster wedding," said Eliza.

"It's not exactly love at first sight," said Aisha sadly.

"It's a shame," said Rachel, "because I thought we might be able to make a dress for Emily, just like my bridesmaid dress. Would you like to see it?"

She didn't wait for an answer, but opened one of the huge wardrobes.

The dress was wrapped up in cellophane. It was made of creamy material, and had a long skirt. We all admired it.

"Though," Aisha couldn't help mentioning, "it's a bit plain."

"What do you mean?" Rachel asked.

"Well, it's *lovely*, of course," Aisha said.

"But I just think a little bit of lace, or maybe a bow—"

"She means it's boring," said Eliza bluntly.

I thought Rachel was going to be offended. But after a moment she said, "I see what you mean. It could be more exciting, couldn't it?"

"Definitely," I agreed.

"Still, it's what my Auntie Izzy wanted. She says she likes —" Rachel thought for a moment — "the *understated* look."

Aisha clasped her hands together. "But, you know, we could easily do a few things to make it prettier!"

Rachel was putting the dress back in her wardrobe. Eliza, Aisha and I started whispering to each other.

"We could do a makeover."

"It would be like sending Cinderella to the ball."

"It's just the kind of thing fairy godmothers do!"

We told Rachel our plan and, to our surprise, she agreed right away. She liked the idea of a makeover just as much as we did.

"And let's *all* get dressed up to do it!" said Aisha.

"Why?" asked Rachel suspiciously. "I thought this was all about *me*."

"Because we're going to be your fairy—"

"Your makeover experts," I interrupted quickly. "So *we* need to look special too."

We had lots of fun dressing up in stuff from Rachel's wardrobe. I wore her white ballet tutu with a crossover cardigan and Eliza wore a summer dress made from pink lace and Aisha chose a pink party frock with sequins. "If only we had our wings," I whispered to Eliza, as I fixed a glittery hairslide in her hair. In the end, Rachel got

114

a bit impatient and said were we going to do this makeover or weren't we?

We helped her into her bridesmaid's dress and then the ideas began to flow! Luckily, Rachel had a craft cupboard that was full of useful things.

"What this dress needs is decoration," said Aisha. "Pass me that cotton wool, Clarinda!"

"Here you are, Araminta," I replied.

"Shh!" hissed Eliza.

Rachel was too busy admiring herself to notice us using our secret names.

We stuck pom-poms made from cotton wool to the bottom of the dress. We glued on flowers cut from silver doilies too. We sprinkled glitter over the top. Then we tried to pile Rachel's hair on top of her head, just like a princess going to a ball – only somehow half of it collapsed and ended up dangling over her left ear.

"Never mind, nobody will notice it's a bit lopsided as long as we put lots of glitter on top," said Eliza, sprinkling vigorously.

"You are going to look like a snow queen!" I told Rachel.

Rachel was still admiring herself in the mirror. Eliza was singing as she worked. Aisha was murmuring the same spell we had used for the love potion:

"Roses are red
Violets are blue
Sugar is sweet
And so are you!"

With every wave of our wands, we three fairy godmothers were using our magic to change Rachel from an ordinary girl into a sparkling princess! The cotton wool we were gluing on was the softest swans' feathers. The glitter we were scattering was sparkling ice drops. The beads on her shoes...

"What on earth is going on here?"

Rachel's mother was standing in the doorway. And she was furious!

Chapter Twelve

"I really don't know what you were thinking of, Chloe," said Mum.

I was at home, having tea with my family and trying to explain what had gone wrong.

"We just wanted to make her look lovely," I said. "And she did. Only Rachel's mum didn't agree."

"She certainly didn't," said Mum. "And I'm not surprised. That bridesmaid dress you covered with glue must have cost a fortune!"

I stared at my fish pie. We'd all thought that Rachel looked a hundred times better after our hard work. But when Rachel's mother had found out, she'd gone crazy! She'd said that Rachel's auntie would be furious and the whole wedding ruined. Then Rachel got mad too. She'd shouted, "If I can't have the dress the way I like it then I'm not going to go!" That hadn't helped.

In the end, Mum had come to collect us and we'd gone home.

"I expect Chloe had her head in the clouds again," said Dad. His eyes were twinkling at me.

"I did not," I said indignantly. Then I remembered about imagining that I was in a fairy tale, turning Rachel into a snow queen.

"Well … maybe just a bit."

"Girls are always doing stupid things," Arthur announced.

I turned on him.

"No, we aren't! No more than boys."

"You are so. Like taking Hammy with you. That was stupid."

"He has a point," said Mum.

"I just wanted Hammy to make a friend! And maybe have some little hamster babies."

"Hamsters are solitary," said Arthur. "Everyone knows that. They don't like other animals – not even other hamsters. Now rats *are* sociable. Haggis would probably enjoy meeting another rat." His eyes started to look thoughtful. "In fact…"

"No," said Mum and Dad loudly.

"What?" asked Arthur, surprised.

"No rat babies!" Mum said.

Dad added, "No hamster babies either."

I got up. "Well, I don't think it's fair," I said shakily. "When humans have babies everyone makes a big fuss of them and gives them cupcakes and says how lovely they are. But when Arthur and me want a few hamster babies or rat babies, which are a hundred times sweeter than human babies, all we hear is no, no, no!"

I ran out of the room and upstairs.

I put on my fairy dress and wings. But it didn't make me feel any better. For one thing, my left wing had never recovered from being made into a kite by Arthur, and it kept falling off. I crouched down next to Hammy's cage.

"We were only trying to help," I told Hammy. "That's what fairy godmothers are supposed to do." But from dropping ice cubes on Mum's head, to our failed love potion,

to Rachel's bridesmaid dress, nothing had gone according to plan.

"Grown-ups never understand anything," I told Hammy. "No wonder Eliza tried to be a bad fairy that time. Maybe we should all be bad fairies... After all, whenever we try to do *good* things it all goes wrong."

At that moment, I wished we'd never decided to be fairy godmothers.

I fetched Hammy out of his cage, and let him run around on my tummy. His claws tickled and made me laugh. I cheered up. And I began to see things differently. After all, we'd had a lot of fun being fairy godmothers.

I heard a phone ring from downstairs.

Maybe, I thought hopefully, it was Rachel's mum, phoning to say she wasn't cross after all. I went out on to the landing.

Mum was in the hall, speaking on the phone. For a while she said nothing much except, "Mmm," and "Uh-huh." But then I heard something that made me feel like somebody had tipped a bucket of cold water all over me.

"*Horse and carriage?*" she said. "Are you *sure*? And then she fell silent as the person at the other end started talking again.

This was terrible!

A disaster!

A catastroff!

"I'm sure it *is* a very nice horse and carriage," Mum said. "But—"

There was a pause.

"*How* much did you say?" asked Mum.

Another pause. Then –

"*Five hundred pounds*!" Mum yelled.

I felt like running and hiding under my bed, but I realized there wasn't any point. So I sneaked past Mum into the kitchen. Dad was doling out dessert. "Is your mum still on the phone?" he asked.

I nodded.

Dad looked at me. Then he pushed some chocolate tart towards me. "Here," he said. "This will cheer you up." Somehow I didn't think I'd swallow even a spoonful. I felt like an enormous slug had come to live in my tummy and was squelching around in there.

"Dad," I said. "Something's gone a teeny bit wrong. Actually, a lot wrong. Actually, it's a catastroff!"

Dad blinked. "You mean *catastrophe*, Chloe, you pronounce it CAT-AS-TROFF-EE. And if you're worrying about Rachel's dress, then don't. I'm sure the dry cleaners will fix it."

"It's not the dress."

Before I could continue, Mum came skipping in and planted a kiss on Dad's cheek.

I stared in surprise. So did Dad.

"What a lovely thought!" Mum gushed. "Of course I've told them no. It's far, *far* too much money. But it was lovely of you to think of it. So romantic – a real, genuine horse and carriage! And I thought that you'd forgotten about our anniversary!" She went skipping off out of the room again before Dad could say anything.

Dad looked very, *very* puzzled. Then he caught sight of my face.

"Chloe," he said. "What's this all about?"

So I explained. About how Aisha had

always wanted to ride in a real, old-fashioned horse and carriage, and how I'd found one on a website and booked it by mistake.

"Don't ever do that again," said Dad sternly when I'd finished. "You must never give out our phone number on the internet." Then he looked thoughtful. "Still, there's no harm done. And your mum really did like the idea. It's a shame it's so expensive – otherwise I really would book it for our anniversary. It could have taken us to a nice restaurant."

I didn't have time to worry about that. I was just so relieved that I wasn't in trouble, and didn't owe anybody five hundred pounds!

Fairy Godmother Tasks

1. Decorate the baby's bedroom.
2. Make a magical love potion (and lose it again). ✓
3. Find a Wild Rose ✓
4. Get a pair of wings. ✓
5. Make a good luck charm. ✓
6. Give someone a magical makeover. 1/2
7. Find true love for Hammy. ✗
8. Ride in a horse and carriage. ✗

Chapter Thirteen

One evening I got a phone call from Eliza. "So what do you think about Sunday?" she asked.

"Sunday for what?" I asked.

"For coming round to decorate the baby's room, of course."

"Whoopee!" I yelled.

"I'll phone Aisha and check she can come too," Eliza said.

She could. After that, we could hardly wait until Sunday.

"I've got loads of stuff," I boasted to Aisha.

"Me too," said Aisha. "Every time I open the wardrobe door it falls out and squashes me!"

With all our bags, it was quite a squeeze on the back seat of Mr Akbal's car. When we arrived, he helped us carry it up the path and we were about to ring the bell when Eliza opened the door.

"Shhh! I've been looking out for you. Let's get this stuff upstairs before Mum notices!"

Mr Akbal left. From downstairs in the kitchen, Eliza's mum called, "Is that Chloe and Aisha?"

"Yes, Mum. We're just going upstairs. Luckily," Eliza added softly to Aisha and me, "Mum likes to rest a lot at the moment. It's because she's so big. If she's down in the basement, I don't think she'll come upstairs."

It took two trips to carry up all our stuff. Aisha had a huge package that needed two of us to manage it. We took everything into the little room that was going to be the baby's. It still had a bare and unloved look.

"We're going to make this place gorgeous!" said Aisha happily. "Let's see what we've all got."

"I've found some lovely cushions," I said, waving them in the air. "They're all fluffy, like rabbit fur. Mum was giving them to the charity shop, so I grabbed them. And—"

"I've got a nightlight," Eliza interrupted. "My auntie bought it for me when we went shopping. She was a bit surprised I chose it instead of a present for me,

130

but it looked so sweet – it's a little log house with hedgehogs inside having their supper."

Aisha was bouncing up and down with excitement. "I've got a Moses basket!"

We were amazed. "A Moses basket? Like one of those cute little cradles?" Eliza asked.

"Yes. Look!" Aisha started to unwrap the bulky object we'd helped carry up the stairs. "It belonged to Abdullah. And then to Ibrahim. And then Mum lent it to my auntie for baby Yasmin. But now baby Yasmin is too big for it, so Mum said I could have it for my dolls ... only I want to use it for *your* baby, Eliza!"

After we'd finished admiring the Moses basket it was time to get to work.

Aisha is the best of us at art and craft, so she was in charge. We had some lovely animal pictures we'd painted, and we'd brought Blu-Tack to stick them to the walls. Soon there was a cat, an owl and a hamster gazing down at us!

"That hamster looks just like Hammy," said Eliza approvingly. Then her face changed. "Chloe! You've got Blu-tack on the carpet!"

"Don't worry," said Aisha quickly. "We'll cover it with this rug."

The rug was one my mum had been going to give away. It was a soft lilac colour and it looked lovely next to the little Moses basket.

"Now let's do the fairy lights," said Eliza.

"I'm going to put up this photo," said Aisha. "I made the frame myself."

Eliza and me couldn't help giggling. It was a photo of the three of us and Aisha had painted in golden crowns, wands and fairy godmother wings!

"We'll be looking down on the baby," I said. "And making good wishes for it while it sleeps."

Aisha got on a chair so that she could put the photo frame on to a shelf. Suddenly I felt her go very still. She was staring out of the window. I craned my head to look, but I couldn't see anything except a blue van at the side of the road.

"What's wrong?"

"Shhh!" Aisha hissed. She looked at Eliza, who was kneeling on the floor, struggling to unwind the fairy lights.

"Eliza, why don't you leave that for now and go upstairs and – and…" Aisha stopped and looked at me.

"Go and choose which toys you want to give the baby," I suggested. Aisha smiled at me gratefully.

"All right," Eliza agreed. "But I'm still not giving it my best toys, like Mr Mouse," she added, as she ran out the door.

"What's the matter?" I whispered to Aisha.

"That van … it said 'decorator' on it."

"So?" I asked. "Maybe somebody is having their house decorated … *oh*." I looked at her. "Do you think…?"

"Let's check it out," said Aisha.

We ran down the stairs at top speed, almost crashing into Eliza's mum who was standing at the front door talking to a man in overalls. "What's up?" she asked, smiling at us. She was really big now, I noticed.

"Please can we have a word with you?" I asked. "It's terribly important."

"Excuse me a minute," said Eliza's mum to the man. She followed us into the hall. "What's the trouble, girls?"

"Is that a decorator, come to do the baby's room?"

"Yes, it is. And just in time too!" Eliza's mum patted her bump.

"But..." Aisha and I looked at each other. Then I burst out, "You can't! *Please!* You see, *we* want to. We've been planning it for ages and we're doing it today, as a surprise!"

Eliza's mum squeezed my arm. "That's so

sweet of you, girls. Such a kind thought. But now, you see, you needn't bother. It's all been sorted. I've picked out the design, the colours, and it's going to look absolutely *perfect*."

She turned away. Aisha and me gazed at each other unhappily. How were we going to break this to Eliza? We turned and trailed towards the stairs.

"I suppose they will do a better job than us," said Aisha mournfully.

I couldn't say anything. I wondered what Eliza would say.

We took a few more steps. And then –

"Wait!" I turned and ran back to Eliza's mum. "Please!" I gasped, pulling at her sleeve, while she turned towards me in astonishment. "I know we won't be as ... as perfect, because it's not our job, but you see ... well ... we just have to do it." I took a deep breath. "You see, *Eliza* wants to. She *really* wants to make the room special. She's even looking forward to the baby now. It's — it's *important*."

Eliza's mum looked at me for a moment. Then, to my big surprise, she bent and gave me a hug.

"Thank you for explaining, Chloe. I understand perfectly. I'll go and tell the decorators we don't need them after all. Now off you go!"

I ran back to where Aisha was waiting. She had heard everything and was waving a thumbs-up sign at me. "Well done, Clarinda," she whispered as I joined her.

"Well done, Araminta, for spotting that van!"

We ran up to the baby's room. Eliza was squatting down, arranging her toy animals in a line against the wall.

"Where have you been?" she asked, but she didn't wait for an answer. "Do you think they look nice like this? I want to have it so that the baby sees them when it wakes up."

Aisha nudged me. "Look, she's giving the baby Mr Mouse after all."

When everything was finished at last, Eliza ran downstairs to fetch her parents. Aisha and I waited, smiling nervously at each other. A moment later, we heard them coming up the stairs.

"What's all this about?" asked Eliza's dad.

"I'm not telling you," Eliza answered in a high, excited voice. "You'll just have to wait and see. Now shut your eyes…"

Eliza's parents walked into the room with their hands over their eyes. Hercules came pattering in after them.

"SURPRISE!" yelled Eliza.

Eliza's parents blinked. They stared around at the Moses basket and the rug and all the pictures, and the fairy lights and a little bowl of primroses and a mobile with dangling stars and all Eliza's cuddly animals lined up against the wall.

"It's wonderful!" cried her mum.

"Stupendous!" said her dad. He looked as if he could hardly believe his eyes. "I wouldn't have thought it possible. All these wonderful things that have suddenly appeared — it's as if somebody has waved a magic wand." (Eliza, Aisha and me looked at each other and grinned.)

"Your baby brother or sister couldn't possibly have a nicer room," said Eliza's mum. "In fact, I would go so far as to say it's perfect." And she gave Aisha and me a secret wink.

Aisha and I smiled shyly back.

Eliza beamed at her parents.

"Of course, *really* you should have done something about it yourself!" she told them. "Instead of leaving it all to us! But we didn't mind, did we, Chloe, Aisha? It's been good fun, hasn't it?"

We agreed.

"I can't wait for the baby to see it," said Aisha.

Eliza nodded. "Me too!"

Later, as we were going downstairs, Aisha looked thoughtful. "Do you know what, Chloe? I think we turned out to be pretty good fairy godmothers after all."

"Do you know what?" I replied. "I think you're right!"

Chapter Fourteen

It was the following Sunday, and Mum was standing in front of the mirror.

"Hmm, I'm not sure about this dress," she said. "What do you think, Chloe?"

Mum doesn't get all dressed up very often, but tonight she and Dad were going to a fancy restaurant for their anniversary. I was going to Aisha's for a sleepover and Arthur was going to Barney's.

"I think you look lovely," I said. "Though

you'd look even nicer if you'd let me do a makeover."

Mum snorted and wrinkled her nose at me in the mirror. "I'd rather not have cotton wool glued all over me, but thank you all the same."

I shook my head. The trouble with grown-ups is they have no imagination. Mum's plain blue dress could have looked really special with a bit of glitter!

"Have you and Arthur packed your things?" Mum asked, interrupting my thoughts. "Remember, you'll need your school clothes for tomorrow." I nodded. Arthur put his head round the door.

"Dad says are you ready yet?" And he looked at me and gave me a secret wink.

Mum didn't notice the wink – she was too busy fixing her hair.

"I'll be down in a minute," Mum told

Arthur, who disappeared out of the room.

"Mum," I asked, "Are you disappointed that you won't be going in a horse and carriage?"

"Well, maybe a teeny bit," Mum admitted. "I suppose our boring old car isn't very romantic. It needs a wash for one thing. But never mind."

I ran on to the landing. I had a balloon of laughter inside me, and I didn't want Mum to suspect anything.

At that moment I heard the hoot of a horn and I hurried downstairs. Dad, looking very smart, was opening the front door. Mr Akbal stood on the doorstep, beaming. Aisha was there too, hopping up and down with excitement. And behind them was a beautiful, gleaming, white vintage car. It had its roof down and everything.

"Wow – that's amazing!" said Arthur from behind me.

"I'm just coming," Mum called and then she stepped on to the doorstep and saw the car. Her jaw dropped.

"Surprise!" we yelled.

Then we all rushed to explain at once about how she'd wanted a horse and carriage, but that was too expensive and wouldn't have been a surprise, anyway. Only then I'd remembered about Mr and Mrs Akbal's new business hiring out  fancy cars and so Dad had spoken with Mr Akbal and it had all been arranged. Arthur and I had been bursting to say something all day, but we had managed not to.

"I had no idea," said Mum. "It's wonderful!"

Mr Akbal took a photo of Mum and Dad with the car, which he said he would send to the newspaper *and* put on his website, and he opened the door so we could all climb in. He was dropping off us children on the way, which meant that we got a ride in the special car too!

"It's a shame Eliza is missing this," I whispered to Aisha.

"Actually, we're collecting her as well," Aisha said.

"Really?" I was surprised. "I thought your Mum said your room was too small for three?"

"She did," Aisha agreed. "*And* it's school tomorrow. But Eliza's parents phoned earlier and somehow she's changed her mind."

We found out *why* she'd changed her mind when we got to Eliza's. Eliza was waiting for us with her bag, and jumping up and down with excitement.

"Aisha, Chloe, guess what? The baby's coming!"

"Ooh!"

"Really?"

"Are you sure?"

Aisha and I could hardly sit still, we were so excited, but Arthur was not impressed. "Huh!" he said. "What a fuss! Anybody would think something important was happening!"

When we got to Aisha's, Mrs Akbal told us we had to calm down. She said it could be a long time yet before the baby arrived and we should sort out our bedroom then go to sleep, just like usual, and we would see if there was any news in the morning.

"This is *so* much more exciting than when Ibrahim was born," said Aisha, as we moved her dolls' house to make space for Eliza and me.

"It's *almost* as exciting as when I got Hammy," I said, as I arranged cushions and blankets on the floor.

"Well, of course it is," declared Eliza. "This is my baby brother or sister we're talking about."

"Remember when you didn't even want a baby," teased Aisha.

"Oh, nonsense!" Eliza said. Then she admitted, "Well, maybe I didn't at first. But that was ages ago!"

Aisha and I smiled secretly at each other.

We knew we wouldn't sleep a wink. We lay squashed up like sardines (Eliza and me on the floor, and Aisha looking down from her bed) and thought about names for the baby.

"Orlando?" murmured Eliza. "If it's a boy."

"I think Alfie would be sweet." I said.

"What about Florian?" Aisha asked. "Or … Eric?"

"It might be a girl…What do you think about Tinkerbell?"

One moment I was lying there, all warm and toasty in my cocoon of blankets, trying to decide on my favourite girls' name … and the next thing I knew I was opening my eyes to see the sun pouring in through the curtains, and Mrs Akbal, with a big beam on her face, handing the phone to Eliza.

Aisha and I waited all agog while Eliza listened. Then she gasped, "Chloe! Aisha! I've got a little sister!"

"Hooray!" we yelled.

Eliza came to school with us and all the teachers made a big fuss of her. Her dad picked her up early and Mr Carter didn't even mind. He just looked all twinkly and said, "This is a very special day for you, isn't it, Eliza?"

Eliza got to meet her new sister *and* she got given a beautiful toy snow leopard by her mum *and* she got taken out for pizza and double chocolate sundae by her dad *and* she was allowed to have some of the presents her mum was given, including a box of gorgeous truffles and she gobbled up every one!

She talked about the new baby all the time. She talked about her before school and after school and at breaktime and lunchtime, and even when I was going to the toilet she stood next to the cubicle door and talked about her!

"I can't wait to hear what she'll be called!" Eliza said. "I wish Mum and Dad would make up their minds!"

Aisha and I heard all about the baby's eyelashes. Her teeny tiny fingers. Her brown hair, just like Eliza's when she was a baby. The way she scrunched her face when she was drinking milk and the burps she did afterwards. We even heard about her pink bottom!

At first we were interested, but then we began to feel a bit fed up. "I must say," Aisha grumbled to me, "I've known lots of babies and I don't see what's so special about Eliza's!" We began to long for the olden days when Eliza spent all her time complaining about the baby coming, instead of saying how wonderful she was.

Then Eliza invited us to go round and see the baby for ourselves.

We tiptoed into Eliza's house while she told us to be quiet because the baby might be sleeping. We waited at Eliza's parents' bedroom door, and then her dad said we could go in. Eliza's mum was drinking a cup of tea in bed and the baby was lying in the Moses basket next to her, because she wasn't old enough yet to sleep in her own room.

We leaned over the Moses basket.

The baby was asleep. She looked more squashed and crumpled than I'd expected. She was quite red. And she was making snorty noises, like a tiny piglet. But then she opened her eyes and squinted at us. And she uncurled a little hand. It looked like a starfish.

"She's lovely!" I said.

"So pretty!" cooed Aisha.

"Isn't she?" said Eliza proudly, as if she'd wanted a baby sister all along.

Aisha and I put our fairy godmother presents next to her on the bed. I'd brought her a tiny teddy bear made of velvet. It was a bit battered, but it had been my favourite when I was little. Aisha had brought her a bead bracelet she had made herself.

To our surprise, Eliza's mum had presents

for *us*. They were very fancy chocolates, in heart-shaped boxes with a bow tied round them.

Then Aisha and I asked what we had both been wondering — what the baby would be called.

Eliza's mum said, "We've decided to let Eliza name her."

(I didn't think Eliza's dad looked too sure about that!)

Eliza was delighted.

"Ooh! Yes! Chloe, Aisha, help me decide!"

"Tinkerbell," said Aisha. (Eliza's dad made a funny noise.)

"*I've* always liked Esmeralda," I said.

"That's a bit too much like Eliza," said Eliza's dad quickly.

"I thought you liked Ariel?" I said to Eliza.

"I've gone off it," Eliza replied. (Her dad looked relieved at that.)

Aisha and I had lots of suggestions.

"Serafina."

"Yasmin."

"Belinda."

"Dorabella."

But in the end, Eliza said, "I know. We'll call her Miri."

Everyone was pleased. Eliza's mum said it was a lovely name and her dad said it could be short for Miriam, which was the name of his favourite grandmother. Aisha said Miriam reminded her of Mariam, which was the name of *her* favourite auntie. I said it sounded a bit like Mirabelle, which was a lovely princessy sort of name and maybe we could call her that if we played pretend games about fairy tales.

Then Aisha and I gave Miri a teeny tiny

kiss and she howled and howled. Eliza's mum said Miri was hungry and if we three girls were hungry too there was chocolate cake in the kitchen.

We ate the cake while Hercules stared at us mournfully because dogs aren't allowed to eat chocolate.

"It's wonderful having a new baby," said Eliza happily. "Mum would *never* let us have chocolate cake usually." She paused. "Actually, I like Miri, even without the chocolate cake."

"You're lucky," I said.

"And she's lucky too," Aisha said. "After all, not every new baby has three fairy godmothers!"

We smiled at each other.

It was true.

Fairy Godmother Tasks

1. Decorate the baby's bedroom. ✓
2. Make a magical love potion (and lose it again). ✓
3. Find a Wild Rose. ✓
4. Get a pair of wings. ✓
5. Make a good luck charm. ✓
6. Give someone a magical makeover. 1/2
7. Find True Love for Hammy. X
8. Ride in a ~~horse and carriage~~ special car. ✓
9. Welcome baby Miri with wonderful gifts. ✓

Fairy Godmothers for ever!

Have you read:

Chloe's
Secret Princess Club

Emma Barnes

Turn over for a sneak peek!

Chapter One

If you want to know about our Secret Princess Club, it all started one morning during Mental Maths. Mental Maths is *really* boring. I often find myself drifting off.

For instance, last week our teacher, Mr Carter, read out the first question and I wrote down the answer straight away. (It was twenty-five.) Then I got the second answer, and the third. This had never happened before! I was so pleased I started imagining what would happen if I got every question right and came top of the class. Mr Carter would be amazed. Arthur, my twin, would be jealous. Our head teacher, Mrs Khan, would give me a Good Work certificate in Assembly … maybe I would even turn out to be a child genius! The trouble is, I was so busy imagining that I forgot to listen to any more questions.

And I came bottom of the class.

That kind of thing happens to me a lot. My mum says it's because I've got so much imagination. My dad just calls me Chloe-in-the-clouds because he says my head is always in the clouds.

So this time, I tried to pay attention. I really did. Only I couldn't stop my eyes wandering about the room, and I saw that the door to the big cupboard-storeroom at the back of our classroom was open a tiny bit. Usually, that door is tight shut. In fact, Mr Carter keeps it locked. So I wondered why it wasn't today.

There must be a reason, I thought. And then my imagination began to whirr...

Maybe the reason that door was open was because it was a Portal to Another World!

If I went inside, who knew what might happen? After all, Lucy got into Narnia by going into a wardrobe in *The Lion, the*

Witch and the Wardrobe. So why not Chloe Higgins of Class 5C?

I was so busy dreaming that I didn't notice Mental Maths had finished and everyone else was handing in their answers. I didn't notice Mr Carter telling everyone to get ready for lunch. Or the lunch bell ringing. Or everyone lining up at the door.

"Chloe," Mr Carter called. "Stop dreaming and get moving!"

I almost jumped out of my skin.

Mr Carter was looking impatient, and my best friend, Aisha, was beckoning me, and Arthur and his friends were laughing at me.

I got up and scuttled towards the end of the line. And then … I didn't mean to do it. *Really* I didn't. But somehow, while everyone else was filing out of the classroom, I couldn't help taking another quick peek towards the storeroom…

… and the next thing I knew, I'd stepped inside.

You see, it's not every day you have the chance to explore a Portal to Another World.

Only … it wasn't another world. It was just a big storeroom-cupboard. A musty-smelling place full of books and paint boxes and ukulele cases and boxes of costumes from school plays.

It was a bit disappointing, because I'd been hoping to go to Narnia and become a queen, the way Lucy did. Oh well.

I turned to open the door. But I couldn't. I'd shut the door behind me. And when it shut — it had locked.

Oh no! I tried again. I banged at the door and shouted, "Help!" Everybody had gone to lunch, though, and nobody heard me.

Oops.

Luckily it wasn't dark because there was a little window high up on one wall. But I still didn't like being shut in.

For a moment I felt scared. To distract myself, I looked at the school play costumes. There were lots for fairy tale characters, and I've always loved fairy tales. I put on a long, yellow wig, a blue dress and a golden crown.

First I pretended I was Lucy when she was Queen of Narnia, and then I imagined I was Cinderella, going to the ball.

Only then my stomach started rumbling. I wanted my lunch! That's when I had an idea. If I piled up all the ukulele cases, I could climb on top of them and reach the little window that looks out on to the playground. I could shout for help again.

It worked! The cases wobbled a bit, but I didn't fall off. I opened the window and leaned out.

"Help!" I squeaked.

The first person to notice me was Rachel, from my class. She was standing close by with some of her friends. It wasn't very nice of them to start giggling. Or to point at me so that other people started pointing and giggling too, until it seemed as if the whole playground was staring at me, Chloe Higgins.

That included Arthur and Mikhail and Barney, who had stopped playing football. And all the kids coming out of the dinner hall (including Aisha). And Mr Carter, who was on playground duty. And Mrs Khan, who was *clip-clopping* along on her high-heeled shoes with a clipboard under her arm.

"Who's that?"

"What's she doing?"

"Why's she up there?"

Even Mr Carter looked puzzled, as if he were wondering who I was.

"It's *Chloe*!" yelled Aisha suddenly. And Arthur said, "Yeah, you're right. What are you doing, Chlo?"

Then somebody (I think it was Barney) shouted, "It's not Chloe, it's *Rapunzel*!"

Everyone screamed with laughter.

"*Rapunzel, Rapunzel*," Barney shouted, "*let down your hair!*"

That's when I realized I was still wearing the long, blonde wig from the costumes box. And the crown. And the ball dress. And that, leaning out of the high window, I must have looked just like Rapunzel.

I could feel my face going beetroot red.

I tried to pull my head back out of the window so I could take off the wig. But I couldn't.

You see, it was a very small window. And

when I'd stuck my head into it – well, it got stuck.

It was the most embarrassing moment of my life. Even more embarrassing than the time I dropped my plate of school dinner on Mrs Khan's foot. (That's why I switched to packed lunches.) Or when I tucked my skirt into the back of my pants and didn't realize (until Barney Big Mouth pointed it out to everyone in Assembly).

Because not only was I wearing a wig. Not only was I locked in a storeroom. But now my head was stuck in a window, and maybe I was going to be looking out at the playground forever!